Praise for *100 Strokes of the Brush Before Bed:*

"The erotic adventures of a sexually ravenous girl . . . A wisp of a book that had a wallop of an impact . . . Readers have simply devoured it."
—*The New York Times*

"A mixture of old soul and sexual newcomer . . . [Melissa P.] brings an emotional authority to her work. . . . *100 Strokes* is by turns romantic, erotic, sensationalistic, and disturbing."   —*Bust*

"Melissa P. is the *ne plus ultra* of an eye-watering literary phenomenon."   —*Telegraph* (UK)

"Catherine Millet can go put her clothes back on."
—*Les Echos* (France)

"Melissa P.'s fictionalized memoir is shockingly frank, explicitly detailed—and, she insists, entirely true."   —*Teen Vogue*

"What's most remarkable about this staggeringly assured debut is not the sexual smorgasbord—voyeurism, sado-masochism, group sex, etc., etc.—but the utter lack of any distractions from sex. . . . A junior-league Catherine M. bound to raise just as many eyebrows this side of the Atlantic."   —*Kirkus Reviews*

The Scent of Your Breath

Also by Melissa P.

100 Strokes of the Brush Before Bed

The Scent of Your Breath

MELISSA P.

Translated from the Italian by
Shaun Whiteside

Black Cat
New York

a paperback original imprint of Grove/Atlantic, Inc.

First published in Italian in 2005 by Fazi Editore

Printed in United States of America
Published simultaneously in Canada

FIRST EDITION

Library of Congress Cataloging-in-Publication Data
P., Melissa.
[L'odore del tuo respiro. English]
The scent of your breath / Melissa P. ; translated from the Italian
by Shaun Whiteside.
p.   cm.
ISBN-10: 0-8021-7022-6
ISBN-13: 978-0-8021-7022-4
I. Whiteside, Shaun. II. Title
PQ4900.P3O3613 2006
853'.92—dc22
2006041135

Black Cat
a paperback original imprint of Grove/Atlantic, Inc.
841 Broadway
New York, NY 10003

Distributed by Publishers Group West

www.groveatlantic.com

06 07 08 09 10   10 9 8 7 6 5 4 3 2 1

To Thomas, who knows how to sniff my skirt,
to my mother the forest,
to my sister the storm,
to my Nonna Madonna.

So go, take the train
'cause if you don't go now, you surely will

—Virginiana Miller, "Elsewhere"

ONE

I threw myself into the streets of the world with a bee in my hair. A bee that buzzed among my tresses, beat its wings convulsively, and buzzed, buzzed, buzzed. I didn't brush it away, I let it build its hive in my head, and everyone who met me said, "You've got hair like honey," and didn't know that there was a bee in my head, rolling around playfully among my thoughts with its soft, bicolored body. And it kept me company, my bee did; it became an indispensable if not very trustworthy companion: sometimes it gave me little bites on the back of my neck that should have hurt. But my bee was too small to hurt me; it left honey in me but never poison.

One day the bee whispered something in my ear, but it was too faint a murmur for me to hear. I never asked what it had tried to say to me and now it's too late. My bee flew away from my hair, all of a sudden, and a passerby killed it. It was squashed. On the white marble I can see a liquid gleaming, a substance: I pick it up with a little spatula and take it to an analytic laboratory.

"Poison," the biologist tells me.

"Poison . . . ," I repeat.

1

Melissa P.

My bee died of poisoning; it wasn't squashed. A few hours before, it had bitten me.

Who's going to keep my silences company? I miss the bee's buzzing; I need its soft whisper. When the morning sun shines, I find my teeth clenched and a sound coming from my mouth: *zzzzzzzzzzzz* . . .

Two ✺

Were you OK yesterday? When you got home and lit yourself a cigarette from the gas ring in the kitchen, when our cat rubbed against your neck, breath quivering, when you shut your eyes and folded your legs like a fetus, what did you think about? Were you OK?

My torments began when I said good-bye to you at the airport, when I came over and said, "So, did you get all that? You check in, go up those escalators and then through the metal detector," and I pointed to it with a finger, "after which you go toward the gate marked on your boarding card, and you're there. Call me when you get home."

That's what I said to you, and then I moved away, came back, and repeated it all word for word. I even repeated my gesture, pointing to the metal detector.

Finally I kissed you softly, our bodies apart, and whispered in your ear: "Thank you."

You, in a voice less harsh than mine, replied, "Thank *you*, darling, thank *you*."

That same evening I made love with Thomas. "Let's do it as though it's the last time," I said to him, looking him straight in the eyes.

He hesitated for a moment, then asked, "What do you mean?"

"Don't be stupid . . . nothing apocalyptic. Just an excess of love."

"Why?" he asked, dumbfounded.

I shrugged. "Because I've had enough of giving myself away piecemeal. I need to stretch to infinity."

"But you always do that," he said.

I shrugged again and snorted.

No, I've never stretched to infinity. I don't know infinity. What I know is boundaries, paralysis, impairment. But not infinity.

"Let's do it this way. Imagine one of us dies tomorrow; imagine that one of us has to go traveling for years and years and then we had to see each other again after a long time . . . or maybe never see each other again. How would you love me, how far would you go?"

He was extremely handsome, I was extremely beautiful. We were warmed by the light from the lamp on the chest of drawers, which bathed our faces with specks of color.

When we made love he didn't exist, but he did exist and so did you. I existed, just an apparition. You and he loved me, tore me apart and kissed me. I saw your nose, his mouth, your ears, and his eyes. I felt two hearts beating rather than one, and when my body surged I shouted, "I love you so, so much," and I was saying it to you as well.

You and he, guardians of my soul and my body. Presumptuously appearing on the terrace of my life, you watch and protect it as I have not asked you to, as I do not expect you to.

His sweat smelled like your neck, and his neck smelled of you. Then it was over. My eyelids lowered like the curtain after a show, and my soft, gratified breath merged with the smells of the room. And you stayed.

You've never made an attempt on my life or my liberty. You're so frail, and I'm too heavy. Now and again I'll have to silence all my theories of life to give more room to that extreme but gentle feeling I have for you.

Maybe you deserve that.

"A one-way ticket for Rome," I said.

The man at the travel agency looked at me and smiled. "Where are you off to this time?"

I looked at him for a moment, tracing every feature of his face inside my head.

"Home," I replied.

He lowered his head as a sign of reverence and, looking up at me furtively, said, "Straightaway."

As he clicked away at the keys of his computer, I studied the brochures behind me. From the Congo to Laos, I could have gone anywhere. From Paris to Hokkaido. From Valparaiso to Athens. Endless possibilities spread out behind me, with many promises and few demands. I could have begun my escape right then, since I was there. But I was scared of the lack of responsibility; it's always frightened me.

"So you've decided on Rome?" the man asked.

I turned around and nodded with a smile.

"Do you want me to make you an electronic ticket?"

"No, please don't. I'd like to be able to hold it in my hand."

It was like suddenly turning in to the road I've seen so many times on the horizon from my street, the one I've been traveling down for such a short time, but I feel as though I've lived a hundred years already, half of those years spent well, the other half so-so, to put it optimistically.

It's always struck me as impossible to reach the point where the two roads cross, so that I've indolently traveled the whole journey without wondering where it would take me and what I would do when I got there.

All of a sudden I've found myself at the entrance to that unknown street, which a gilded sign identifies as "Likely Street. You can go straight ahead or turn left."

So I looked back and saw my footsteps leading to the place where the parallel lines of the street joined in a perfect perspective: the tarmac was half destroyed, ruined by hail, rain, the wind, cratered and worn to the thinnest of crusts. I saw trails of blood where people had fallen; here and there I saw corpses lying naked and gaping. No trace of you. Just hints of a mammalian smell that spread along the lifeless, deserted street. I took another look at the gilded sign: it looked like the entrance to paradise. But someone once told me that there is no better paradise than your own personal hell (or perhaps my conscience told me that, to give me an alibi?). In any case, I decided to tempt fate, and rather than continue along that gray street, which I reached by passing through a black hole shouting, "Light! Light!" at the top of my voice, I sniffed the air and turned left, holding both hands crossed over my heart.

I took the airline ticket and held it delicately with two fingers: my ticket of entry.

As I left the agency, a thin line of cold made my skin ripple. I wrapped myself up in my overcoat (the red velvet one, the one Ornella thinks looks like a dressing gown) and climbed the street called the Acchianata di San Giuliano. I decided to pass by Piazza dei Crociferi, where the excess and luxury of the baroque vie with the degradation, death, and decomposition of the graffiti-scrawled houses, with flowers inexorably sprouting and withering from their stones. That's where I had my first kiss, where I came to blows with some half-wit; farther over is the staircase where, one evening, I sipped a beer with a boy I didn't know, who didn't even ask for anything in return.

But no memory reawakened sensations that had been covered over by time.

So I went down, down as far as Piazza dell'Elefante, and all I saw were the gray coats of the council workers.

I walked on toward the fishmonger's, and even there the only thing that came to mind was that time many years ago when you, Grandmother, and I came here to buy fish, and I was struck by the sight of that starfish on the back of the swordfish, still alive. A few, a very few memories, most of which are pointless and faded now.

If someone asked me which city I hated the most, I would say Catania, and I would give the same reply if they asked me which city I loved the most.

You've always told me that being far from your own land is the most painful thing imaginable. You've always told me that if and when I went away, homesickness would grab me by the throat and drag me down into a pit of sorrow and despair.

I told you that as far as I was concerned, one place was pretty much the same as another, and actually Catania was the place I feared most, because Catania swallows people up.

Darkness, ash, lava cooled and congealed. In spite of the sun forever peeping among the baroque reliefs and the white lace curtains of the old houses in the center, the whole city seems plunged in a big, endless, abysmal gloom. Catania is dark. It's as though it were sliding into a vast, gaping mouth, being pulled by an exhausted train. Catania's even like that when it seems that life can't be contained by its small squares and its stone-scratched streets, at night when young people, bag snatchers, whores, drug addicts, families, and tourists all arrange to meet in the same place, at the same time, leading to exotic, chaotic orgies. Catania is beautiful because it has no hierarchies, because it has no time, because it is unaware of its fascination. It's beautiful like a naked woman, white-skinned and with black, black hair, opening her eyes wide when a brute clamps his hand over her mouth, hissing, "Don't breathe, you whore."

That's what Catania is like, a whore who doesn't speak, because someone is suffocating her.

I am a deeply Catanian creature. I have both life and death within me. I'm not afraid of either, but sometimes my life tends toward death.

Often I hear people who have been away from home for too long being told that the only thing drawing them back to their own beds is the need to take possession of their own roots, to eviscerate the earth and reappropriate their roots. Roots? What the fuck kind of roots are they talking about? We aren't trees; we're human beings—human beings who have sprung from a seed and remain seeds for all eternity. If anything, the only place we have ever put down roots is in the womb.

And, if one day I want to return back to my origins, if I want to eat my roots, I'll just have to rip open your belly, climb in with my whole body, and bind myself to you with a cord that is nothing but a fiction now.

But it wouldn't do me any good. I want to go on being a seed. I want to be my origin and my end, and I don't want to rot in the ground, any ground; I want the wind to carry me forever. I don't want ordered spaces.

It isn't really spring yet, even if technically it is. The sky is still so wintry . . . and the faces of the people are wintry, too. The Colosseum stands dramatically at the heart of the city, its fat ass in the middle of the road, exposed to everyone. I try as hard as possible not to look at it when I go shopping. I don't like the Colosseum. It looks like a middle-aged man trying to convince everyone of his virility, even though he lost it ages ago. I can't bear it. It wears me out. I walk down the noisy street, bags in hand and eyes lowered; I walk so fast that by the time I get to the front door my calves are hard and tense and my fingertips are sawn in half by the plastic bags, fat and swollen like a pack of sausages.

I suckled on the Catanian nipple for too short a time; perhaps I was weaned too soon, but it was what I asked for.

What did I do with all those years, in that dark, cramped chasm? How could I have failed to notice that Catania was taking over my soul, when I hadn't even granted it permission? Why didn't you tell me?

Did you conspire with the city to make me stay there forever, clinging to your breasts? You constantly told me that I would be homesick for my city and my family, that if I went elsewhere I'd find loneliness and conflict, and that there's nothing finer than waking up in the morning and feeling the sea breeze stinging your nostrils. I don't care: I hate the sea and I'm really fond of loneliness and conflicts.

Shame, though, that you got it wrong.

Sorry, I'm being harsh. I've always had a deviant vision of other people's thoughts; perhaps you didn't think all those things. But perhaps you hoped them, just a bit.

THREE

I didn't love him, I felt no tenderness for him, I wasn't particularly fond of him. I exploited his adulthood, his experience, the security he was able to give me.

He exploited the childish part of me that I guard so jealously, because it's small, insignificant, soft, and yet precious. We exploited our bodies with the excuse that we were freeing our souls. He said I had given my freedom to him, that with me he felt like a falcon. But what had he given me?

I gave myself to him because he was the only one at that moment in time who could lick my wounds. Lick them, open them up, and make them burn. And then lick them again.

I told myself that his body was exactly the same size as the deep abyss that had formed inside my own. I thought his body, stretched out on top of mine, might suddenly heal the bloody wound that opened up a little more each day, each day another centimeter.

Then I let him love me, and he let me love him.

At the precise moment when I came, I already felt sated and full, and wanted to be alone with myself. He turned his back on me and I curled up in a fetal position on the bed, closed in on myself. I masturbated.

Then he left me alone and stayed motionless on the unmade bed, completely naked, one arm over his head and his eyes fixed on the ceiling, lost in thought. His body still pulsed with erotic discharges, his virility a powerful presence.

In those moments of silent stillness, when the darkness of the hotel room was lit at intervals by the headlights of passing cars, I wondered what he would be left with if the natural perfume in which he was drenched were assimilated, swallowed, fixed within me. He would become an arid oak tree, about to die of dehydration, and his roots would be firmly planted in the earth, but the sap would no longer course through that rough and imposing trunk.

Four

There's a sofa, and the soft blue light from the television screen. The sofa is covered with a pale fabric patterned with big brown flowers, and I'm wearing a tartan blanket. I'm four years old or maybe younger. I've spent the whole day with my father, and we've been watching the elections of the new president of the Republic. I haven't the faintest idea who he is, but Oscar Luigi Scàlfaro is a nice name—it sounds pretty. It reminds me of my heroine, Lady Oscar. You're in bed with a headache, Dad soon joins you, and I'm left alone on the sofa, listening to the music of the cartoon, whispering, "Lady Oscar, Lady Oscar, the blue of your eyes holds the rainbow . . . your sword . . . in battle . . . don't ever change, don't ever change . . . Lady Oscar . . ." My eyelids close heavily.

I fall into a deep sleep, not at all disturbed by the flashes from the television.

Someone is lying beside me, zapping the TV with the remote control.

An itch in my legs wakes me all of a sudden, my eyes are half closed, and in a voice still thick with sleep I ask, "What are you doing?"

Another voice replies, "Don't worry, I'm just checking to see if you've become a lady."

I go back to sleep, immersed in a field of brown flowers that Lady Oscar is elegantly felling with a clean sweep of her sword.

Blood drips from the stem of a flower.

FIVE

I awake with a start, drenched in sweat, the sheet wrapped around my legs. I'm almost tangled, trapped as mosquitoes are trapped in tears.

Thomas is lying beside me; he's gone to sleep with his glasses on and with *Il Manifesto* in his hand. I slip off his glasses, turn out the light and tell him I love him, lay my head on his chest and feel his heart squeaking, like a malfunctioning mechanism. Not regular, human beats, just a squeak, an attempt to stay alive. My first thought is this: until a few months ago, his heart would have exploded at contact with my face. Now it squeaks. What do you need, I wonder, the grease of love?

Back in Catania: I was dressed the way Claudio liked, and I didn't mind going along with his aesthetic tastes and his desires: I was the one he desired. The fact that I liked him was neither here nor there, because pleasing him was the most important thing. We were sitting outside, at the table of a restaurant just behind Piazza Teatro Massimo.

Summer was just over, and autumn was softening the faint tan that colored my skin. The streets were calming down after the chaos that had become a constant lurking presence in the cobbled streets. The table stood at a slight angle in the uneven street. Reggae music filtered from the restaurant, and I couldn't help smiling when his face assumed an expression of amazement: I was well aware that this kind of music was as remote from him as it could be. He would have preferred somewhere discreet, a setting to which he could have applied adjectives like "delicious," "exquisite," or "charming." He would have called this place "noisy," "vulgar," and "young." But all he did was look at me and recoil from this place as best he could.

"It's extraordinary how you manage to make me say things I've never said even to myself," he said.

I just smiled. I wasn't listening to him.

"When I talk to you about my ruined dreams, about the new life you've given me, for the first time I feel as though I'm not being judged. As though someone thinks highly of me. Do you understand what I'm getting at?"

I nodded, looking utterly bored.

He stopped talking for a few minutes and then, gazing at me intensely, asked, "What do you think of me?"

The last thing a man should ever do is ask me what I think of him.

I don't think anything—what's to think? If I love you I love you, if you disgust me you disgust me. Is that so hard to figure out? And you want to know what I think? I think you shouldn't give a fuck what people think of you. I think you're selfish and cowardly, and blind, too. I think you were so greedy for me that you didn't even feel, while you were fucking me, that my body was as motionless and unresponsive as the expensive white wine in this big glass.

He looked at me with big eyes, like a whipped dog. He waited.

I took a sip of wine and replied, "I think you're a good person."

"You know, I've never felt free. Not even with my wife," he said, not paying the slightest attention to the words I had just uttered.

I didn't feel like talking. He felt like talking. I let him go on.

"I always have this vise around my heart, my brain, and my tongue, making me passive and powerless. Do you have any idea what that means? Do you?" His voice had grown reproachful; it was as though he were telling me off.

I shrugged and said gently, "No, I don't know. I've always loved my freedom."

His lips trembled and he went on, more violently than before. "You're a little girl, and there are some things you can't understand. You don't know what it feels like to be deprived of yourself, to see your own dreams carried away by rational, conscious, adult people! I was like you: I didn't want to grow up, I felt free. But someone ripped me off. And they'll rip you off, too," he said, clenching his teeth.

"That's one point of view," I replied.

"You don't know a thing, you haven't a clue how I feel."

No, and I don't want to know.

"I do know, Claudio. But please, don't keep going on at me about this."

"What do you want to hear? That life is beautiful, that people love you, that it's all one long funfair?"

I smiled broadly and exclaimed, "Why not?"

He started to cry, his voice growing muffled. Tears spilled from his eyes and trickled down the rough skin of his face.

I looked at him compassionately and whispered, "Everything will be fine. We should go home—you've got to calm down."

He nodded and moved away from the table without saying good-bye.

Left on my own, I went into the café and smiled as the music bounced off the walls.

A hundred times good night.

Six

His eyes were unsteady; they looked as though they were drenched with tears, they looked stunned, fragile, malleable. And yet they raped, they crushed, they pleaded, they reproached.

The parked car in a country lane at the feet of Etna, the rain that had finally stopped crashing against the windshield, the smell of rotten earth, my panties and stockings scattered around inside the car, my hair heavy with damp, his penetrating breath, and the smell of his aftershave. The tissues on top of the glove compartment, the purple, yellow, and red colors of the flowers, the trucks passing behind our heads, the bee convulsively striking the window. Sweat, saliva, and humors, the stench of damp fabric, the clink of his belt, the sun timidly reappearing, passion, haste, anxiety, jealousy, impotence, inconsistency, illusion, lies, indifference to the point of grief.

Everything was there, everything but love.

SEVEN

My skin turned transparent. All of a sudden all my pores opened up until my body became a single great pore. My body like glass. My face, too. My veins, my arteries, my capillaries. I can see everything. The red and purple highways crisscross to form a beautiful cobalt blue. My ovaries are two little chickpeas suspended in midair. One is bigger and lower than the other, because of my period, which is due any minute. Inside, a red and lumpy pulp churns around like juice in a juicer. My kidneys are two beans, just as I imagined them when our teacher tried to explain their shape to us in primary school. I'm starting to think of my body as a vegetable garden. My lungs are coated with black moss, here and there, and the white splashes are rare now, rare but very beautiful.

My heart. My heart pulses, veiled by a nylon stocking, like the ones bandits wear. A little condom with life inside it. A bandit on the run from death but also from love and the extremity of pain. Because too much death has lain in wait for him, too much pain has buried him, too much love is strangling him.

21

My brain. My brain. My brain. Nothing but dreams. Many photographs and no sound.

When I was in the car with you and Dad, lots of things came into my head. I loved the car journeys we took; I liked driving all around the coast of Sicily, admiring the landscape that passed alongside us while infinite quantities of thought-molecules wrought havoc in my little brain. It was surprising how the coastline changed over a distance of only a few kilometers: from sand to cliffs, from cliffs to rock pools, to sand again and then, unexpectedly, to hills. A big, green hill ending in a sheer drop to the sea.

I woke first and we set off early in the morning. I couldn't bear you waking me up, I didn't want to get in your way. So I got up and washed and by the time you woke up you found me clean and neatly dressed. It was quite normal for you to find me already up and ready—you never paid me any special compliments. Perhaps if I had a child I would praise him, every now and again, just to make sure he didn't feel unwanted . . . to avoid making him feel incompetent—that's it. While Dad never even noticed what I was wearing, you studied me for minutes at a time.

"Why did you put on that skirt? It doesn't suit you, it needs washing." "What are you doing with those shoes? Going dancing? Put on a pair of sneakers . . . wear the ones from last year, the dirty ones. We're going to the seaside, to Grandma's. We're going to spend Easter there."

And yet, on those trips, I felt fine. I left the window closed because I hated the wind filtering through the window of the moving car . . . it felt like a sword sent flying through the air, or a cowboy's lasso. I liked the sound of the radio and I liked the sound of your voice when you spoke to Dad. From Mia Martini to Mina, from Riccardo Cocciante to Loredana Berté: those were the sound tracks to my thoughts. Those songs you used to sing at the top of your voice, the songs I learned by heart, whispering them shyly because I was ashamed of my hoarse, masculine voice. Loves shattered, lost, abandoned: those were the themes of my childhood. I often fell asleep. It was amazing, sleeping in the car, enclosed in an artificial belly kept alive by an engine. I almost felt as though I were returning to your womb. How did it feel to have me inside you? Did I feel like an intruder, or like part of you? Did I weigh that much? You've always been so small, so tiny . . . didn't having another life inside you hinder your movements? And did you ever talk to me? What did you say?

Only yesterday I asked Thomas to suck my breasts as though he were sucking milk. Lately I've been feeling maternal all the time. Anything that makes me feel like a woman is a blessing.

Seriously: you know what I thought during those long, long journeys? I thought, One day I'd like to publish a diary, I'd like to write about my life. I really need to think about keeping one . . . even if I know I would quickly get tired of writing.

One day I asked Dad to give me a nice diary with a big lock. For a week, every day when he came home, I said, "Dad, have you got the diary?" I always asked him when we were having our dinner, always in a low voice, and I asked him when the table was already plunged into silence—I didn't want to interrupt you. Every time I asked him if he had brought the diary I felt guilty. When he said no, I wasn't angry: it was the most obvious answer to such an indiscreet question. If he had brought one home, he would have given it to me straightaway—what was the point in my asking?

Weeks later you took me with you in the car, you let me out, and we went into the store. The skeletal lady behind the counter, the one with the boiled-fish eyes and the fine, fine hair, was the mother of one of my classmates in primary school: I liked her, she was like a fairy dressed up as a witch. All my schoolmates were afraid of her, while I actually thought she was beautiful. You pointed toward a shelf with notebooks, pencils, pens, and other kinds of writing equipment: a diary had been thrown in the middle. The cover was smooth and white, a dirty white, with a picture of a blond girl in a leather jacket sitting on a motorbike. The diary was very thin—there couldn't have been more than twenty pages in it. And the lock looked extremely fragile, golden and covered with little brown stains. It was the only one they had. It was a leftover from the eighties. Although it was horrible I was extremely happy and absolutely loved it. The fairy disguised as a witch charged you fifteen hundred lire for it.

But my usual capriciousness soon led me to abandon the project. I wrote only five pages before I got tired.

I'll write when I can't help saying something, I promised myself. I hated to write anything meaningless.

So, when I thought the moment had come to bury my soul and keep only my material alive, pure and lewd, some perverse angel whispered in my ear, "Write. These emotions will never return. If you write, a scrap of soul will be left in your breast."

I never had anything to lose, and in pretending to keep a diary I ended up writing a novel.

EIGHT

This evening, as he laughed, I noticed that one of his teeth overlapped with another, as though shyly hiding. I found this defect incredibly fascinating and wondered why I had never noticed it before. I know his moles and his skin, and I know the different smells that arise one by one from the exploration of his body. I know that he has an extra rib, the one he didn't give to the woman. He has freckles on his back and big, deep knuckles on his hands. The gleam of the stars is a flat, monotonous glare in comparison with the flash of his eyes. He has a soft mouth, the kind only women tend to have. He has a maternal belly and breasts, soft as the limbs of a newborn child.

He has a mole under his eye, in the same place as mine.

As I looked in delight at that twisted tooth, he stared at me and asked, almost irritably, "What's up?"

I knew something was wrong.

I knew I was about to be abandoned.

The first thing we shared was a book of poems by Mao Tsetung, bought in an antiquarian bookshop. We read it at night, in his room, our warm, naked bodies covered by the duvet. Red Christmas lights hung from the walls of the room, and we thought we were in a transparent cube suspended in mid-air, from which we could be seen by anyone.

NINE

They put us outside beneath a damp, watery sky. All we had to shelter us were a few umbrellas—gas heaters our sole source of warmth. A very bright light was angled toward our table, and the smoke from the roasting meat clung insolently to our hair.

I wanted to go, I wondered what the hell I was doing there.

"Meeting important people"—that's what my condition requires me to do. But my mind and body mutiny.

As far as I'm concerned, the people sitting around this table, assailed by the damp and the smell of roasting meat, aren't important. I couldn't give a crap about that actor; that editor can go fuck himself, thank you very much; that photographer can squash herself into one of her own pictures and live inside it forever.

This is what all we humans do: we stay trapped inside our creations, our worlds . . . and no one can save us from our worlds, no one can drag us out of them.

While they all raise their glasses to my success and a thousand more to come, I repeat just one thing in my head: Go fuck yourselves, the lot of you, you horrible ass-licking cunts.

I'd just like to see the look on your faces if I showed you my pussy.

I grip Thomas's hand as I whisper to him, "Take me away from here, now."

TEN

I'm eating salted crackers. Over there, some delirious jazz pours from the stereo and outside it's raining. My hips are so wide you can rest your elbows on them.

My voice is hoarse. Massimiliano was here this morning, that Neapolitan friend I told you about a few times: sometimes he comes to see me and when he smiles I can't tell if he's sad or what.

"I'm frightened," I whispered to him.

He looked at me compassionately, embarrassed, and said, "Of what?"

"I'm frightened that he might betray me . . . ," I replied.

"What makes you think that?"

"Nothing . . . it's just a feeling."

He looked at me and nodded, and I immediately understood what he was thinking.

I screwed up my eyes as tightly as I could and screamed, "Do you think I'm crazy?!"

He said I was getting reality muddled up, that the world I thought I lived in wasn't the real world.

"Open your eyes, Melissa. You're creating a reality that has nothing to do with the reality around you."

I took him by one arm and hurled him out, with such violence that a scrap of his checked shirt stayed in my hand, torn out by my furious fingers.

Then I shut the door behind him and felt dizzy for a moment. Exhausted, I went to the bathroom and noticed that in my haste I had left a blood-filled Maxi Pad in the basin. It doesn't matter; blood doesn't bother anyone. I went out onto the balcony; the washing machine had finished its cycle. I stood and looked inside the drum for a while—I don't know why. My head is so full of thoughts it seems empty. I'm sated with happiness, happiness is exhausting me, demoralizing me. I ask myself every day, every moment, if this happiness will end and when. I'm too apocalyptic, I know. And maybe masochistic. Yes, I'm well aware of that. The messages sent by the world are exasperating: nothing lasts forever, everything comes to an end, everything withers, everything dies. And if it didn't happen to me, well, what about that? If I stayed this age forever, if I remained intellectually ignorant, if I stayed in love forever, what about that?

I know, I can't accept change. I'm too much of a traditionalist, too attached to my memories and, paradoxically, attached to fantasies about the future. That's why my present is so restless, even if it's happy: I mix the past, the future, and the present as though an exquisite sweet might emerge from the dough. A sweet that does you good because it hurts. A sweet that's good because it's full of clashing ingredients.

There is nothing positive in this wealth of feelings. It's an orgy, Mum. An orgy of feelings . . . in which it's impossible to work out who's winning, in which you can't predict whether the ultimate winner will be death or life, pain or love. It's an infinite chaos, bound by many little interlocking rings that have slipped into my throat, dragging me to places that are never the same, to more and more exasperating states of mind.

I'm disturbed to the depths of my marrow. I don't know how to hold back my instincts; I allow myself to be corrupted by my obsessions, by my most violent passions. Do you think it's just because I'm Sicilian? Or is it because I'm fucking terrified of losing the most beautiful part of me? Of losing Thomas?

ELEVEN

I shook him awake; I was breathless.

"There are ghosts, I can hear them," I whispered so they couldn't hear me.

"A dream," he said, "a bad dream, calm down."

No, I couldn't. I really did hear that hand striking the wall opposite the bed. It beat out a rhythm, creating a sweet melody. Through half-open eyes I had seen a tall, black female figure.

Go to sleep, go to sleep, don't be afraid. Go to sleep, go to sleep, don't be afraid. Don't be afraid.

This morning the memory of the night has already passed, but a strange attraction leads me to long once more for the black darkness. I hear a weird echo, I sip the careless milk of my thoughts, my legs are naked and crossed, I look impatiently at my cigarettes, because seven hours without smoking is far too long.

The stench of the dirty dishes in the sink grows from day to day. This morning I decide to clean the house; I swear I'm going to do it. I'm serene, even if that echo sounds like a Tibetan chant that won't leave me alone.

He says, "Come and see."

With my lips open in a smile, I go look across the narrow corridor, and I think this morning I really do feel like making love. I think that when I go into the room I'll throw him on the bed and fuck him without even looking at him. He's just had a shower and he's damp. I can already feel the skin of his feminine back brushing against my fingertips.

"Come and see," he repeats.

I don't go in. I stop in the doorway, with one leg against the wall and a smile that hints broadly at what I have in mind.

He doesn't notice but points at the wall.

A black hand. Or, rather, not a hand—three fingers. Three black fingers imprinted on the wall, as though someone had set fire to his own skin and then pressed it against the plaster.

I just say, "I told you so," and feel something clenching inside me, and someone tells me that I have to hide because no one knows how to listen to that echo.

TWELVE

I realized I was in love with him one late summer evening. An electric evening, in a Rome that was colder than usual, turned in on itself as though to apologize for making too much noise, for being too beautiful, too schizophrenic, too old. The Rome of emperors and usurers, of politicians and tax collectors, lost girls and girls in miniskirts and stilettos, the Rome of vineyards and dairies, churches and brothels.

Sipping my Vin Santo, I studied the images running across the screen. The TV enfolded and contained me, and for the first time the eyes and words of the scarecrow presenters were directed at me, like rough-edged swords waiting to be used. What was I like? I wasn't. I wasn't me. I was a caricature of myself, I was the most exasperating version of myself, I said all the things I would never have wanted to say, because what I want to say is too crazy and too confused for anyone to understand. I was only pretending to cope.

Martina and Thomas were lying on a big leather sofa; Simone and I had our eyes glued to the TV.

"Tommy, would you give my back a rub? I'm aching like a beast . . . ," said Martina.

He brought his cigarette to his mouth and held it tightly between his lips, letting it dangle. He kept his eyes half closed to shield himself from the smoke that brought tears to his eyes; his long eyes, with their almost girlish lashes, looked even longer, two crescent moons.

Martina turned her back to him, and he started rubbing her vertebrae with two fingers, strong and extremely delicate. I thought about how good it must be to have two big hands like those on your body, and the smoke from his cigarette filling my nostrils. At that moment I desired him, and not just physically.

At some point I even thought of asking him, "Thomas, would you rub my back, too?" and I swear I nearly did.

But I don't know how it happened . . .

That very evening, on an enormous Empire-style bed, Claudio lay on top of me and I halfheartedly opened my legs. By now I was wearing nothing but a black silk bra.

The smell of old wood gave me a comforting sense of warmth. The darkness engulfed everything. I was wearing the necklace with the pearl that you gave me, the only spark of light in the room. My thoughts were like long, long shooting stars whose tips I couldn't find. Claudio's attitude toward me was a mixture of jealousy and envy, and if I didn't dedicate enough time to him he was hurt and made me feel guilty. He cried on the phone, begging me not to leave him, mortifying my happiness. "I can't wait for this dust cloud to settle," he said. "I want to have you all to myself. And don't kid your-self, they'll forget about you soon enough."

No, Claudio, I'm not kidding myself. I hope deeply that they do forget me, that no one remembers me . . . and you, Claudio, you've got to forget me, too.

Claudio entered me and started moving back and forth. I felt my swollen belly, and felt his penis as something strange now, something unfamiliar. I turned my head to one side as I felt his abdomen rubbing against my pubic bone.

With my nipples erect I wanted to torture him.

After five or six thrusts he usually started sweating, water pouring from his forehead. When he was on top of me, the drips ran along his face and reached my lips, and I licked them wearily away with my tongue: they were very salty and bit-ter, with a vague taste of sperm.

That night he didn't get as far as perspiration, because at the third thrust I stopped him and said, "I'm in love with some-one else. I can't do this."

He broke away from me without a word, and I turned to face the other side of the bed. In front of me there was a huge mirror framed in an old wardrobe, and I stared at myself for a few moments that felt like an eternity. I studied myself and saw once again that same lost, passive expression that has accompanied me throughout my life.

"You aren't in love with someone else, you're in love with your success, and you think I'm a hopeless fool who's barely capable of satisfying your whims," he whispered a few minutes later.

"Please stop," I said quietly, tired of hearing him say that success had altered me. The only thing that had changed was his vision of me; I felt that he was hostile and saw me now as something that belonged not to him but to everyone. I was starting to despise him—not hate him, but despise him.

"It's the writer you met at that party, isn't it?"

"If that's what you want to think, go ahead and think it," I replied indifferently. "I'm stupid as always . . . I always tell you everything. But things are going to change from now on, you'll see," I said, facing away from him and speaking very quietly.

I heard him crying but shut my eyes. I couldn't have cared less about his victimhood.

He just cried for a while and soon worked out that it wasn't going to move me. His tears flowed whenever he needed someone to give him a little understanding. I wished him black with bruises from my fists, white from my withheld caresses. With my nipples erect, I wanted to torture him.

The sheets rustled faintly, and before I realized what was happening I heard a croaking sound. I looked at the mirror on the wall in front of me and saw in its reflection that the sheet behind me was slightly raised, and that his hand was gripping his penis. Lying in bed next to me he was masturbating, partly in order to come, but also partly, perhaps, to take his revenge on me.

I felt him touching himself and shut my eyes; I tried to sleep and feel nothing more.

With my nipples erect, I wanted to torture him.

He got up and went to the bathroom, from which I heard his final, long moan of pleasure.

The next morning we had breakfast in silence. I never saw him again.

In a sense I felt like an orphan, though one with two fathers: a natural one, for whom I have never felt anything, not rancor, rage, or love; and one whom I had taken it upon myself to love and on whom I had imposed the task of loving me.

With my nipples soft, freedom arrived.

THIRTEEN

I'm naked at the computer; he's in the kitchen washing the dishes and whistling. I like noise when I'm writing—I like a racket. He puts on a CD and I, still writing, find myself moving my hips and making my revolving chair move back and forth. The curtains aren't closed yet and the windows are high, typical of a seventeenth-century palazzo. Everybody can see us, and we're happy for anyone to watch us making love. Perhaps that's typical of people in love: showing everyone you love each other. I wander along the corridor, brushing the walls with my fingers. I enter the sitting room and stroke the bonsai tree, standing on tiptoes. He has his back to me, and I wrap my arms around his chest and start rubbing my pelvis against him. I turn him resolutely around, look at him coyly, aware that I've made a movement he likes. I turn around, rub my ass against him, and he delicately strokes my back; I sit down on the edge of the cold, wet sink, the contact makes my whole skin shiver, and my body swells upward.

He takes me there and then, grandiosely stretches his body out on top of mine, and whispers words I like into my ear, warming my earlobe with his breath.

Then I hear a coughing fit and open my eyes: I see a woman leaning over the table, coughing convulsively; she looks up and smiles wickedly at me. She's blond, wearing a flower-patterned dress, and she's thin and coarse. I look at her for a moment longer, then I look at him, close my eyes, open them again, look back at the woman and see that she's disappeared. I can still hear her coughing. I draw him toward me and devour him.

His tongue bleeds, dripping red on my neck.

FOURTEEN

Lovely, absolutely lovely—that film was fantastic. A touch of genius in that shot.

And what do you think of the new director in competition at the Berlin festival? And Cannes? And Venice?

Well . . . I . . .

And what do you think about Edgar Allan Poe, about Céline, about the fin de siècle poets? Don't you think their words blend perfectly with their ideas?

Yes, of course . . . but . . .

And did you see the Paul Klee exhibition? And the Tintoretto? Did you see Tarantino's latest, and Buñuel's first?

No . . .

Your brains are in a state of collapse. You all know how to know. I don't.

I'm a Homo sapiens who hasn't evolved yet. I'm still in the initial phase and I intend to stay here.

They're all motionless pillars of ash. Compacted ash, impossible to break. I'd so love to walk on their soot. Their stillness frightens me yet, at the same time, fascinates me.

Someone once said that we're surrounded by dead people. Dead people walk in the street, eat, drink, make love and read lots of books and see lots of films and know lots of important people. But dead people, unlike living people, can't have palpitations; they can't have emotions. They use only their intellects, their minds, and they tend to show off their own culture.

I'm scared of dead people.

I'm scared of the thought that one day I will die, too.

At the beach at Roccalumera there was an enormous NO SWIMMING sign, and yet it was the most crowded beach in the whole of eastern Sicily. There was no sand, there were no rocks. Just pebbles. Pebbles that got stuck between your toes, that dug into your tender skin.

"Here, put on your rubber shoes so it won't hurt," you said.

I always hated those horrible rubber shoes. They made me feel ugly, like one of those old German tourists with little white hats and those inevitable rubber ballet shoes.

I preferred to hurt myself, and when I did a lot of walking I even ended up liking the sensation, that gentle torture that I inflicted on my childish skin.

I didn't like going down to the beach in the morning; the ideal time for me was early afternoon, straight after lunch.

"You can't go swimming, not right after lunch," you, Grandma, and my aunts all chorused, while the men inside snored, back from their night's fishing.

"No, I swear, I'm not going to go swimming. I'm going to lie down in the sun," I said seriously.

"You'll get sunstroke!"

"I'll wet my head every now and then," I replied wisely.

I set off with all the paraphernalia, accompanied by Francesco and Angela, who had previously dispatched me to persuade you to let us go.

We crossed the street, the three of us hand in hand, and once we reached the shore, we threw the inflatable mattress into the water and lay down on it. We played at betting who would get their belly wet first. The water was extremely cold and it felt as though all the food we had just consumed was freezing in our stomachs. After initial unpleasant experiences, we had grown used to jellyfish. Around here they're small but lethal. We brought olive oil, Nivea Creme, and butter, mixed them all up together, and greased the places where we got stung. In contact with these substances, our skin fried like bacon and eggs. Then we put a hot stone on top, gritted our teeth, and beat our feet on the ground.

Francesco, small as he was, managed to impale the jellyfish with his dagger. On the water's edge there were dozens of decomposing jellyfish, melting in the sun and giving off steam.

While he was cruelly killing jellyfish on the beach, Angela and I ran in under the shower, sure that no one could see us. We let the water run over us and sang the theme song from a television music program: "Brancamen-ta! Ta-ra-ta-ta . . . ," we crooned, writhing like snakes in a bowl.

You and my aunts arrived at about five o'clock. From a distance, washed out by the sultry air, you looked like characters from a Sergio Leone film. The heat, the silence all around, you armed with your fighting gear: sunglasses, cushions for your backs, hair bands, eye masks, sarongs, transistor radios, Tupperware containers full of biscuits, fruit, and *panini* made with oil, tomato, and salt—my favorites, the ones that burned my chapped lips.

We looked at one another from a distance and felt like thoughtless beasts, instinctively assessing an opponent's weak points. After a few minutes you started running and shouting at us, "You scoundrels, you've been swimming, haven't you!"

"Eight wasted years! You're eight years old and you've wasted them all!"

"I'll have your soul, you wicked child!"

"Mum, how are you going to take my soul?"

It seemed a lovely image, you making a hole in my stomach and pulling out my soul with your hands, as though it were a rope.

We felt an exponential joy: the joy of our aquatic play and the joy of transgressing your stupid rules. Why . . . if you didn't want us to go swimming after eating, why on earth did you bring food to the beach?

At seven o'clock, when the sun started shrinking and the sea turned gray, down came Grandma, the Boss.

The Boss was no taller than us children, she had short fair hair, big green eyes, her skin was smooth as silk, and her breasts were worn out from having six children in as many years, her belly swollen and hard. And her thighs . . . the most beautiful thighs I have ever seen. Slender and sleek, without a hint of cellulite, toned and soft.

The Boss came down to the beach even more heavily armed than you, with jars of water, trays full of food, boxes of ice creams, and big bunches of bananas. The Boss filled us with awe, and we were forced to eat the bananas beneath her gaze.

"Eat it up for your Nonna, it'll do you good."

At the eighth banana, if one of us said, "That's enough, Grandma, I'm full," she cast you a glance so grim that you wet yourself, and it was a good thing our swimsuits were wet already.

Our stomachs became endless storehouses of food—we could have kept going for months. It was her way of expressing her affection.

Then, down came Dad and my uncles with their own gear: cameras and movie cameras. They said they wanted to photograph us children, but in fact their lenses were always trained on the bottoms of the women in the sea. You got furious, but still you took the sun, mumbling, "What's so lovely about that bum, what do they see in it? It's flabby, sagging . . ."

Every weekend the band came and set up in the central courtyard surrounded by the villagers' houses. I watched it all, sitting on the concrete step, letting my legs dangle because I couldn't touch the ground with my feet. There was Signor Sibilla, who, when his wife went away, flirted with his neighbor, a fat, vulgar woman who gave off a strong, rancid smell. Then there was the Witch, who came down covered in sequins, her eyes surrounded by gleaming, green eye shadow, her black, black hair down to her shoulders, always wearing tight, fluorescent clothes. She sat down next to the band's keyboard player and tried to follow the music so she could play the songs on her *pianola* the next day. She was our band for the rest of the week.

Grandma's thighs, on these occasions, were sublime, especially as she danced. "Put your hands in the air, shake them all about . . . Do it when Simon says, and you will never be out."

They were sublime both to me and to Signor Loy, the Sardinian who looked like a tarantula. Every weekend the band had to leave earlier than planned because Granddad started punching Signor Loy, who, undaunted, went on slobbering over Grandma.

Queen of the summer, she was more radiant than the rest. She gleamed, and her brilliance was more powerful than the sun's reflection. More glittering than the Witch's sequins.

Fifteen

Sometimes I think about you. No, that's not true, not sometimes: I think about you all the time. And every time I do a tear slips out, from only one eye. If Thomas asks me why I'm crying, I reply that it's nothing, that I've focused my eye on a point on the horizon and that's why my iris is stinging. I'm thinking about you and your unbroken solitude.

The pizza has just turned up and you've been searching through the money box to find coins because the boy has no change. When he (and his pimples) have disappeared, you laugh and say, in Sicilian dialect, "*Che scemu carusu*"—"What a stupid boy."

You sit down on the sofa with your legs crossed and switch on your TV, trying to find a film that might move you. A costume drama, preferably, with a tight, romantic plot. Francesco and Morino are sniffing at the tomato on your pizza; you hold out a little bit of sauce on one finger. You've already opened the windows, the terrace with the little garden is a few feet away, and you catch the freshness of the newly watered lawn. It's lovely to see Ornella lying on her belly on the carpet, head on a cushion, face pointing straight at the TV. But her eyelids are closed—she's just gone to sleep.

I love hearing her tell you to fuck off when you call her to go to bed, to get between the sheets. She rises to her feet, looks at you with her direct, imperious eyes, and says, "You're a fucking idiot, why the hell did you wake me up?"

You don't reply, because if you did the two of you would come to blows.

If I'd been with you, I would have sat still with my cheek pressed against your bottom and would soon have gone to sleep. But now you're alone and the cats have followed Ornella between the sheets.

You've lit a cigarette and sat yourself down in front of the television again. Your eyes, which are made of water, are drowning in an ocean of tears.

When you wake up, you realize that it wasn't my voice calling you but the infuriating crackle of the umpteenth unextinguished cigarette making the umpteenth hole in the same old sofa.

You go to bed knowing that I wasn't calling you and you weren't able to get pissed off and say, "What the hell do you care if I sleep here on the sofa?"

You slink off to bed, tears drying on your cheeks.

I'm in another world, falling in love.

I think about me, about you, about him, about me and him, especially. Your eyes are made of water, mine of fire, his of earth. Out of the three, I'm the one who can endure your dominion, the one who loves it.

Sixteen

I advanced, slowly at first, and then, once I had managed to touch his thigh with my knees, my movements became even more enveloping. I circled him lightly with an arm. His body stiffened and his breath seemed to falter for a few moments. He stayed motionless, blocking off all contact with the world. With my outstretched little finger I gently touched his erection. It was powerful, yet incredibly light. I had never touched a real erection before. That was why my hand moved higher and higher until it reached his heart. When he lightly brushed my fingers, I realized that nothing would be as before.

"Do you want to sleep with me tonight?" I asked him.

We were at Cosenza in Calabria, and the university where I was staying had put two rooms at my disposal, one for me and the other for my companion.

"It's horrible sleeping on your own . . . ," I went on, plunging further and further into my embarrassment.

"OK," he replied, his cheeks growing fiery.

The smell of his neck was intoxicating, he was young, he was a child. He was everything I wanted.

"The scent of your breath . . . ," he whispered suddenly in the night, "I love the scent of your breath."

I clutched his T-shirt with my fingers and closed my eyes.

He imprisoned my breath in a glass jar, and he sniffs it every time he makes love with me.

SEVENTEEN

The train's progress accompanies our movements, our sighs creating a light and liquid countermelody with sudden surges of emotion, our lips brushing, a race to kiss each other's bodies, tongues darting disturbingly, imperiously, the night's darkness, broken here and there by street lamps scattered along country roads, reconciling troubled fantasies and provocative imaginings, my thighs gripping his body, pressing him tightly, as I cried out to him, "You'll never want to go! Why are you getting away? Why won't you come back? Why won't you suck my breath?"

My palms against his warm, maternal body, my neck thrown back, my eyes holding back their tears, perhaps tears of blood.

The echo has started whispering in my head again, too faint to be properly understood, but loud enough for me to perceive a breath of wind, the north wind. All of a sudden I came, giving off so much energy that he too felt an electric shock in his belly. Blood, blood everywhere. Blood in my head, blood in my eyes. Empty, my veins.

Then I trace a line with the fountain pen my father gave me, the one I use to write with; I want to work out whether I've still got any blood inside me. Empty, completely empty.

I just remember him going back to his cabin and shouting. I remember his dirty fingers and his forlorn and distant eyes.

Distance, one day, will take him to the very rim of the segment of our life; he will go far from me and end up in *her* arms. When he is with *her,* mists will rise up and thicken, and keep him from remembering. While he is with her, I will die slowly, allowing myself to be dragged along with those mists. That way at least I'll see him from close-up.

A poisonous tapeworm nests in our bellies; the slides of our life are printed on its body. Each time the tapeworm moves, a slide settles underneath our navel, and the light projected outside enchants us. We stand and stare at it; then we burst into tears.

At first I couldn't work out what it was that stirred in my belly. I thought it was a child that didn't want to grow and didn't want to be born, a child that wanted to stay immersed and suspended in my amniotic fluid. But then I saw images in my head, and those images were born of pain.

That pain was born of the movements of my entrails, my guts, my flesh.

A pain with its own roots in my past, which I can't cough away: I have to live it and I have to watch it.

The tapeworm helps me do that, the tapeworm loves me.

Eighteen

The sea was rough and I was four years old and wearing a red swimsuit. The beach was scorched by the early afternoon sun; the pebbles gleamed and stood out against the intense blue of the sky. Around my waist I had a plastic rubber ring with a pattern of red apples. I held it up with both hands, stamping my feet because I wanted to swim at all costs, even though the waves seemed determined to swallow everything up.

"I want to swim!" I shrieked, tears pricking my eyes.

My father, lying on his mat, pretended not to hear me.

"I want to swim!" I repeated until he was forced to look up at me impatiently.

"Well, you can't," he said. "The sea's too rough."

"That's what I like about it," I replied. "I like playing with the waves."

Lying on your stomach and sunning your back, you muttered, "Go on, let her do it, go on, as long as you're there nothing will happen."

Inside I was smiling with satisfaction, but my face was still furious.

I ran toward the water's edge, still holding up my rubber ring. Dad caught up with me, I put one foot into the water and it was terribly cold, but I didn't care.

"It's cold," he said, "let's get out."

I said nothing but just kept walking until the water came halfway up my belly.

I headed toward the open sea, my toes no longer touching the bottom, and now the waves were dragging me and my rubber ring. Behind me, my father was growing impatient with my saying, "Dad, let's go."

I swam and played with the waves that buoyed me, high and majestic. Perhaps I was smiling. They were like big arms that lifted me up and then dropped me back down again, and for a moment I felt a mixture of fear and delight. Fear of drowning, and delight at being lifted toward the sky, just for a moment, just for a second. I felt myself being rocked.

I turned around and saw him, so impatient now that his face was almost contorted with pain.

I felt so much sorrow at that moment. I saw his wet trunks and I thought it was bad that he was feeling cold. I saw the pained expression on his face and felt so much tenderness; I chastised myself for being selfish, for thinking about my games.

"Dad, let's go back to the shore."

He practically ran out of the water, while I floundered impetuously, battling against the waves that seemed more and more intent on carrying me out to sea.

With my eyes narrowed slightly, I tried to get closer to him but I couldn't. I still said nothing, because I didn't want to see that expression on his face—I had to do it on my own.

By the time I reached the shore, he was already lying on his mat reading the paper.

NINETEEN

Last night I had a beautiful, disturbing dream. I was in it, with Thomas and a little girl. A beautiful little girl with red hair, a round face, and a pair of red, fleshy lips. I was almost frightened at the sight of her; her beauty was disconcerting. She was our daughter.

But in the dream I was at once myself and Thomas and the girl. I could see with everyone's eyes. I felt part of everyone.

We were dressed in nineteenth-century clothes. Not the sumptuous nineteenth century of the courts but the nineteenth century of the ordinary villagers.

The little girl takes us to the sea. She makes us immerse ourselves in the waves, but we don't swim.

We stay suspended underwater for a long time. Around us there are octopus, jellyfish, lobsters . . . the little girl is lying suspended above the void, her arms along her hips and her long, long red hair still growing and flowing beneath the water. Her hair is beautiful and silky, and it grows and grows. Then, at some point, her hair turns white and bristly and starts to shrink back until it finally disappears. Now her head is bald. She's a newborn baby, but she is still surprisingly beautiful.

I kiss her, I press her to my breast, and she shuts her eyes and lays her face on my neck.

An icy sensation woke me up. I touched my neck and it was extremely cold. That lasted only a few seconds, because I shut my eyes again and went on with my dream. The little girl has died in my arms and I have floated to the surface, passing through a cave. Thomas stays down there, looking at her and kissing her. But I have left only in a physical sense, because I'm still seeing through Thomas's eyes. He picks up the little girl, rises to the surface, and when he reaches the cave, he lifts her into the air and cries, "She's alive! She's alive!"

You, dressed all in black, run and shout with joy. I go on looking at her beautiful face, and realize that she isn't alive at all. She's dead. But I pretend she's alive. We all pretend she's breathing.

One day I will inhabit my dreams and have a great orgy of love with all the people I love, all the people I have loved.

TWENTY

"Do you want to?" the man asked me.

He was tall, quite sturdy, with two burning black eyes and curly black hair that thinned over his forehead.

He was holding out a half-open wooden box with one hand; in the other he held a hundred-Euro note and a slim box cutter.

I stared at him and imagined that he was the chief of an African village, simultaneously offering me the treasure of his land and handing me the sacrificial dagger with which I was to cut my finger and mingle my blood with his.

"It's really good, excellent stuff," he went on.

I imagined the men of the village digging the dark, dry earth to remove the precious, crystalline material.

He gestured to me to accept his gift.

I stared into his eyes and saw he wasn't really there. He saw me, but he wasn't looking at me.

He wasn't fully in control of his faculties, and he didn't understand that he was looking at a little girl who was barely of legal age and who looked at least four years younger than she really was.

I shook my head.

He smiled at me and tipped his powder onto a silver tray, splashed here and there with a few drops of champagne. He wiped away the droplets with his shirt cuff and muttered something.

All of a sudden he sniffed. He raised his head and threw it back and closed his eyes, twitching his nose like a rabbit.

For a moment I thought I saw his body turning transparent; I saw his skin melting and his internal organs becoming visible. They were darker than his eyes, and here and there the mucous membrane was torn by an ulcer. The crystal powder spread all the way through his body, branching like a river into different streams, and it looked almost like a divine spring, a purifying fountain.

Then a large belly appeared, followed by the rest of the body of a beautiful woman, who walked over to African-chief-guy and stroked his hair, asking him if it was good.

He took a deep breath, widening his nostrils, and replied, "Divine."

The woman pulled a face, as though to say, "A shame I've got a brat in my belly, otherwise . . ."

Then she looked at me and asked me, "You've never tried it, have you?"

I shook my head and answered, "No, I don't like it."

She nodded, walked toward a big chest of drawers, opened one of them, and took out a joint, already rolled.

She looked at it as I might look at a particularly fine penis and then she sighed.

She lit it and lay back on the bed, smoking with gusto.

A few weeks later I saw her acting in a film; her hair was longer and she didn't have the belly yet. Her pupils were tiny pinpricks.

Twenty-one

It happened all at once. I was sitting on the toilet and felt first an itch in my ovaries and then a dull splash in the toilet bowl. When I was little I was convinced that frogs could come out of the toilet and climb up my back. I lifted myself up from the bowl, holding my legs wide, and blood dripped to the floor.

There were no frogs in it. There was a tadpole. A human tadpole. It was red, floating in a golden swimming pool, looking at me with its one black eye, which was almost bigger than its own head. With a little tail, its body was elongated like a lizard's.

"*Suttu 'n palazzu c'è 'n cani pazzu, te pazzu cani stu pezzu ri pani,*" this disgusting creature whispered, a nonsensical tongue twister in the Sicilian dialect of my childhood, something about a mad dog and a piece of bread.

I felt my heart tremble and my thoughts blurred. The tadpole swam there, moving back and forth as though enjoying its aquatic game. I could hear the shrill laughter of a child in the distance while the tadpole went on swimming and swimming, repeating its curious phrase.

Then, afraid that it was a monster, I flushed the toilet. A mighty whirlpool dragged it down to the sewer.

Because of the noise of the water I didn't hear Thomas arrive. He had closed the door and was putting his bag on the ground.

"I'm home!"

Grabbed him. That's what I should have done. Grabbed him and strangled him.

"Where are you hiding?"

Strangled him with rage, with keen love, with the love that made me love him for an infinitesimally short length of time, and for the death that he dragged from my belly.

"*Pequeña* . . . where are you?"

I came out of the bathroom, looking at the floor, and smiled at him.

"What were you doing?" he asked.

"I was in the bathroom," I replied.

Lick away the blood and hold him naked and clean under the pillow.

"Hey, listen, I've brought you a surprise . . . !" he said enthusiastically.

Touch his soft limbs and plunge a finger into his chest. Rip out his heart and lift it to the sky.

I know it took two of us, but I put up no resistance . . .

Attach him to my nipple for a few minutes, long enough to weep.

Then I felt a hairy head stroking my calves and for a moment I thought my son had returned in the form of a velvety ghost.

I looked straight ahead and asked Thomas, "What is it?"

He stared at me and then he said, "It's a dog . . ."

I lowered my head, eyes full of tears.

And then I burst out crying.

The darkness had already entered the room, and the red curtain floated slightly in the breeze, while the noise from our neighbors' TV filled the still silence.

"What shall we do?" he asked me, stroking my feet.

"He's already done what had to be done. Everything's just as it was," I replied crisply.

He got to his feet, lit a cigarette, and went to look out the window. I heard him breathing.

The cowering dog took refuge in a corner and followed all my tired movements with the corner of its eye.

"Everything's just as it was," I repeated.

The smoke from his cigarette rose in circles and dissolved in the air.

"Why did you throw it away?" he asked me in a tone of voice that I had never heard him use before.

"It came out all by itself, I . . ."

"No, no," he broke in, "why did you flush the toilet?"

I stopped and thought for a moment, because I didn't really know either.

The dog went on staring at me, and that phrase echoed around in my head: "*Suttu 'n palazzu c'è 'n cani pazzu, te pazzu cani stu pezzu ri pani.*"

"Perhaps out of fear," I replied.

"Fear of what?" he asked me.

I shrugged, but he couldn't see me.

"You should have shown it to me," he said.

"What difference would that have made . . . ," I replied, tears beginning to sting my eyes again.

Then he turned around and said, "I'm sorry."

Everything's as it was.

Is everything as it was?

Twenty-two

You're almost black and I'm white as a Q-tip; you're cheerful and I'm melancholy.

I remember your yellow car very clearly: a yellow Fiat 127, an old model you never see around anymore. It was funny, it looked like a cartoon, and we were the main characters. You had a raincoat the same shade, canary yellow. For me you were "the lady in yellow." You had two earrings that looked like sweets, yellow and soft with a slight dip in the middle. I watched them as you drove. I looked at the mole behind your ear, the mole that identified you as *my mother*. You were that mole. Without that mole you wouldn't have been yourself, not even with the yellow raincoat and not even with the sweets in your ears.

After lunch we stayed on our own and played like two sisters only a few years apart. You spoke to me and I listened to you. You spoke to me because while I was listening to you I was serious and moved my head as though to say, "I understand, don't worry, go on."

You told me so many things, Mum, and none of them are in my head now, but perhaps they've taken root in my soul.

Afterward, when you were tired of talking, I asked you, "Mum, where are we going today?"

You shrugged, giving me a trusting smile, and said, "Who cares? Let's just get in the car and see where it takes us!"

That yellow 127 was enchanted, it always took us to different places, and to me those places were enchanted, too. Anonymous places, deserted, gray squares, the houses of chattering and theatrical relations, the beauty parlor run by your best friend, the one you exchanged important confidences with, thoughts about marriage and husbands. Sitting on a stool, I studied your body, covered with creams and oils. I can still smell their perfume—I only have to think about it.

Your words and your friend's words have remained fundamental for me: I think it was in that room in the beauty parlor that my sexual journey began. I think it was there that I first heard talk about men and first began to form any sort of an idea about them. I was all ears, I was always discovering something new, some new curiosity was always being satisfied. Every day, when I asked, "Mum, where are we going?" I hoped you would say, "To the beauty parlor!"

The 127 was our nest, our refuge. From what? Time, perhaps. You were twenty-five or maybe even younger, and I was nearly five, but we both sensed that time would steal something very precious from us: our levity.

When you swapped the yellow 127 for a red car, our relationship changed, and I was forced to go alone to the enchanted places, the places of illusions.

* * *

"Tomorrow your daughter will be able to walk the roads of life alone, the roads woven of tears and dreams, and perhaps her wound will be in her heart."

Do you remember those words?

I remember them. Every day.

Twenty-three

"I'm going to buy some cigarettes," Thomas said as he left, slamming the door behind him.

I was smoking the last one, lying on the sofa, transfixed by the pictures and the voices on the television. I nodded, looking straight ahead.

When I heard the elevator door opening and closing again, it was as though a flash of lightning had suddenly passed through me and filled me with superhuman energy. I ran to the window and grabbed his mobile phone from the sill.

Frantically fingering the keypad, I dash through the messages in his in-box. There's nothing there to give me any concern, although for a moment I have a sense of foreboding that he might have put another girl's number under my name or his mother's. Then I run through all the texts of the messages and that hint of foreboding fades away.

Suddenly a loud cough right behind me makes me start, and I feel the air stirring my hair.

I turn to see a woman behind me and say, "What the fuck do you want? I'm busy. This isn't the time."

The woman smiles at me and whispers in a croak, "I like

what you're doing. You've got to know everything. Go on, go on checking his every move, follow his every footstep and listen carefully to his every word: he could be lying to you at any moment. I'm here to help you, to make you realize that reality isn't as you imagined it; it's actually very different."

"Really?" I say contemptuously, "and what would you know about that?"

She doesn't reply but goes into the kitchen and pours a little water into her glass. Without saying a word, she turns toward me and inverts the glass of water. To my astonishment the water doesn't fall to the ground but instead follows a precise and perfect horizontal line. A line that stops a few inches from my nose.

I look at the woman and ask her in amazement, "What is this?"

She folds her arms and, with a smile, replies, "This is your reality. Transparent, resolute, fluid. You poured it out where it seemed most appropriate to pour it, and now you're living in it, but the space in which you've liberated it isn't one that belongs to you. What you see before your eyes is your reality, your true reality, in the place where it should be: in a perfect straight line flowing in different directions simultaneously. That line is you."

"So what you're trying to tell me is that I've made bad choices? Is that it?"

She shakes her head and comes over to me, sending ripples through the water that still hangs over the room.

"What I want to tell you," she says, "is that until now you've concealed your true nature because you're attracted by the idea of a peaceful, normal life. But that isn't what you want; it never has been. And what you're doing now, checking up on him, is a sensational gesture on your part: the first in a long series. That's why I say to you: enough of this nonsense, take a good look at what's in that bloody mobile, and think hard about what you find."

The rapid stream of words makes her cough again, and while the convulsions make her tremble and twist, she disappears. She fades away.

The little stream that floated a few inches from my nose vanishes, as well, while the sounds and the cold of the room are heard and felt once more.

Not upset in the slightest, as though I had just opened the front door to a neighbor asking to borrow a couple of lemons, I go on running through the fascinating data supplied to me by that diabolical little machine.

A new name jumps out from among his incoming calls: Viola. So who the fuck is this Viola?

All of a sudden, sweet but forbidden features appear in my mind. Two long, well-manicured hands, two slender, agile legs supporting a perfect bottom. Suddenly the woman of his dreams appears before my eyes.

A thin, pungent layer of fear insinuates itself between the folds of my muscles. My mouth contorts and begins to tremble, while my heart thumps harder and harder. The cold of the

Twenty-four

One is tall and thin, with a burned face and a brown shawl that completely envelops her. She shows me her wrists and they've been slashed.

The other is small and blond, with blue eyes, a purple hat, and a purple shawl. She looks like a circus performer. Her legs are stumps.

A mother and a daughter stand hand in hand. The daughter has a white dog that she's holding by the collar. The little girl's name is Obelinda and she's wearing a brown floral blouse buttoned up to the neck. Her mother is almost identical, although her eyes are a different color. They have gassed themselves.

A Turkish couple smile; they look as though they have just emerged from their own wedding. They're happy and content; the woman's wearing a pretty pink dress. I saw them smashed against the wall by a car.

When my soul returns to my body, my head is heavy and the first thing I think is: what death do my ghosts think I have died?

Twenty-five

As we watch a comedy film that doesn't make us laugh, Thomas tells me a dream he has had.

We are sitting at a sumptuously laid table with a brilliant white tablecloth, and the courses have been arranged in an elegant and orderly fashion. Pouring some red wine into a glass, I clumsily knock it over, making a purple stain that spreads across the white cloth. Then I start crying, saying, "I'm sorry, I'm sorry." He kisses me and tells me it's nothing, that it could just as easily have happened to him. He demonstrates that he's equally capable of spilling his wine on the tablecloth and making a stain. But I go on crying, saying it's all my fault. His stain covers mine and he says, "You see? No one will notice, the whole tablecloth's dirty now."

He falls silent and looks at me without speaking.

I know he's afraid. I know he knows that I'm afraid. We both know that this bloody fear will kill us. I'm too weak to kill him because, in the end, I like fear. But I like the desire to go on loving him even more.

*   *   *

Today, once again, he left without saying good-bye. And yesterday he came home without a surprise present: no ice cream (he used to bring me an ice cream almost every evening, with loads and loads of cherries), no film from the video shop, not even a kiss.

Yesterday as he was brushing his teeth, I came into the bathroom without knocking, and I saw him kneeling on the floor peering into the toilet bowl.

"What are you doing?" I asked him.

Embarrassed, he drew himself upright and replied, "Nothing . . ."

I immediately understood the cause of his unease and, at the same time, his curiosity.

"I flushed it away," I said. "There's nothing to see."

"I know, I'm not crazy like you," he said cruelly, slaying me with his eyes.

As in the first months of our affair, we aren't making love. Back then, abstaining before immersing ourselves in each other was a wonderful erotic game, though. Now it's a source of unbearable pain, but I know it would be much more unbearable if we actually did make love. It's as though his awareness of my sexuality has shrunk and is starting to crumble. I no longer want to fall in love with him, to be inside him.

His body was like a musical instrument. He was a marvelous grand piano, studded all over with white and black keys, and my fingers started playing it fearlessly, and yet they moved clumsily. I had no score, but his sighs and the light in his eyes told me that my melody bewitched him.

His body was a perfect contrast, his thick, burgeoning eyebrows spread out like a patch of hair allowed to grow at will. And his penis was a perfect fusion of angelic candor and devastating demonic power.

"You don't love me anymore."

"Is that a question?"

"No," I answered.

"You're the one who's stopped loving me," he said.

"What's destroying us?" I asked him.

"We are," he replied.

"Go if you're going," I said.

Twenty-six

Now I know who Viola is.

All those weeks she's had him many times, and she's made love with him in every position, and I saw them having a coffee, hand in hand, during a lunch break. Her laughter constantly changed and his body transformed itself like soft clay into a body that was different every time. And he loved her on every occasion, whatever face or voice she was wearing that day.

I met her yesterday when I went into the pet shop where she works. She's young, she isn't beautiful—I don't think any of the others are really beautiful—but I do think she's his type, I'm convinced she could be. My first impulse was to hit her and kick her without losing my temper, coldly, deliberately. Strike her on that tight-fitting top, beneath which jutted two enormous breasts.

A man called her by name from the other side of the shop and that name was Viola.

I gritted my teeth as though I wanted to break them.

She looked at me sweetly and said, "Are you looking for something? Can I help?"

If you really want to do something, help me to take away those horrible images that are rooting themselves in my imagination. Please put your panties back on and get off that sofa; arrange your hair and twist it into a braid, reapply your lipstick and do up the zippers of your boots. Put on your scarf and your coat. And before you walk through that door, don't say good-bye, just whisper, "This is the last time we'll see each other. It was nice—you're marvelous," as you look at him lying there, powerful and naked, wondering why you're leaving.

And when you go through that fucking door don't cry, love. Don't cry—that would hurt me too much. The idea that those big green eyes of yours might never again see the light of the sun, because I would have blinded them with the light of my fire.

Viola looks at me, while with startled eyes I watch the whole scene of my film play itself out.

"You're Melissa, aren't you?" she asks.

I nod and reply clumsily, "Yes, why?"

"I've seen you on TV a few times. I like you." She goes on smiling. What the hell are you smiling at?

"And I've read your book," she goes on. "I really liked it, although I'd have written it differently myself . . ."

Go fuck yourself, bitch. Go on, just show me what you would have done. Take a piece of paper and a pen and write a book, if you're capable of it. But all you're capable of is straddling the dick of the man who belongs to me, who will never give himself to you as he gave himself to me.

"I don't need anything, thanks. I've got to go now," I say as I make for the exit.

She watches me going without a word, and I know perfectly, I CAN SEE THEM, I see that her eyes have become a boundless green marsh that will soon, very soon, swallow me up.

TWENTY-SEVEN

Only a few weeks had passed since that night in Cosenza. Thomas and I were on a train taking us to the place where we would celebrate New Year's Eve on our own.

"Do you have any idea where we could go?" I had asked him.

"A quiet place," he had answered, "far away from everyone."

So we had rented a little house surrounded by trees, lost among the Umbrian hills. It was red as a cherry, small and red.

There, we said, our dreams would meet at night, regardless of where we ourselves might be.

"When we're far away from each other, our dreams will be there, and they'll meet—we'll see them twining in the air and they'll dance in a close embrace to a symphony that hasn't yet been composed," he had said.

Inside, the house had yellow walls and terra-cotta floors, and if we walked around barefoot we could feel a vague, faint warmth spreading around the whole of our bodies.

Once inside, it was almost impossible to leave. I think a thin, poisonous cloud hung in the air above the bed and kept us from getting up. Three days passed as though the hours, the minutes, the seconds, the day, and the night belonged to other galaxies, other worlds. In that suspended red world, above the great green breast of those hills, the only thing that quivered with life was love, a gigantic, lost, stunned love. I sipped slow and long, and I gulped it down, a love that allowed us to stroke each other and sometimes to kiss, but never to plunge into the deepest, blindest darkness of passion.

His body was soft and motherly; I stretched myself out on top of him and was no longer afraid.

"If we were ever to part," I said, "who would I tell my funny stories to? When something funny happens I can't wait to tell you about it."

Who will I tell my funny stories to now? And do such funny things really happen?

I don't know, I don't really think so.

Perhaps what I flushed into the sewers wasn't something human, but the fruit of an extreme feeling whose name I've forgotten.

Twenty-eight

At four o'clock this morning I was woken by a voice that led me to the study. It was the woman in brown with the slashed wrists.

I looked at her, frightened, and she grinned crookedly.

Often, during my nightmares, I have felt an oppressive weight that keeps me from screaming, from calling for help, from running. The same thing often occurs to me in reality as well, and it happens when I can't keep track of myself and my ghosts.

"Pick it up," she said to me, nodding to the pen on the desk.

I didn't move.

"I said pick it up!" Her narrow lips didn't move, but I understood.

"What do I have to do?" I asked her, half frightened, half curious.

"You know what you've got to do. Don't be an idiot and pick up that bloody pen—hurry up."

I picked it up and held it as though holding the metal probe of a scientific instrument. I clutched it very tightly.

I went over to him. He was asleep, the sheets wrapped messily around him without covering him up. His lips were half open, his feminine eyelashes very, very long. He looked like a beautiful little girl.

His chest was bare, so I brought the tip of the pen to the skin, with the intention of tearing it. And then eating it and not digesting it.

I brought it a little closer and my eyes filled with tears. I pressed the pen against his chest, but I didn't plunge it in. I let a drop of blood color his white, white skin.

I remembered a line from a song: "Maybe it's not quite legal, but you look great covered in bruises."

I woke him up to make love. To heal his wound.

And mine.

And the deeper he plunged, the more he healed me; the more he healed me, the more ashamed I grew, the more I longed for death, the more he said he was waiting for it.

When he made love to me, pressing me close, drowning his love and desperation inside my madness and desperation, I heard a Sicilian voice call, "*Iettiti, Vora, iettiti*"—"Blow, north wind, blow." All my madness floated to the surface, stimulated by my echo. Not the kind of wind that cleans and refreshes but a wind that brings with it detritus and ancient breaths, ghosts, and memories.

Then I disappeared.

Then he disappeared.

Twenty-nine

I remember that in our sitting room was a grotto and in the grotto was a statue of the Madonna.

I remember that she was bleeding and that the child she held in her arms was bleeding, too.

I spoke to her and you came in from the other room to ask me who I was talking to.

I didn't listen to you and went on talking in a language you didn't know.

You had a word with Father Pasqualino and he told you to try to record my voice.

You did, but when you played it back the tape was blank.

Then you talked to Dad and he hit you and then he cried, admitting that that morning he himself had seen a man walking unperturbed through the kitchen.

You went to see Father Pasqualino again and he came the following afternoon to bless the house.

As we walked him to the gate I started running and shouting that there were dozens of snakes coming after me.

Then you took me to a psychologist and he told you that I was suffering from depression and hallucinations.

I was five years old and didn't know those words.

You told me that depression was deep sadness and hallucination was deep euphoria.

When you told Dad what the doctor said, he hit you again and then he broke all the windows in the house.

I remember that in the years that followed, you brought me to your friends' houses and made me walk through all the rooms, asking me which were inhabited by spirits and which were not.

I pointed to the corners of the house and then I fled.

Until the age of eight I often saw a shadow dashing past me but I could never make out what it was.

I went back to the psychologist and he sent me to a psychiatrist who told me to make my madness bear fruit as a way of freeing it.

I drew, but I couldn't color anything in without going over the edges.

I bought a guitar, but I was afraid that the strings would cut my fingers.

I wrote and something inside me moved.

I wrote, I wrote, I wrote lots and lots, and then I became famous.

And the thing I had freed came back and invaded me.

Killing me.

Thirty

Once, you and I went for a walk in the country. I had a long stick to help myself climb steep slopes, and every now and then I cynically squashed any lizards that passed close by.

You were pregnant, and your belly was hard and swollen. I was worried that the lizards might hurt you; I was afraid that the whole world might hurt you. So I protected you with my little body and followed you everywhere you went.

We stopped to sit under a big magnolia with white flowers. I remember that the sap spilled from part of the trunk and I stuck my finger in; under the magnolia was a tiny pond in which we bathed our feet. It was spring and the world seemed like Eden.

Countless butterflies and dragonflies swirled suspended between heaven and earth; it was as though they wanted to keep us company but never found the courage to come too close.

"You see those?" you said, pointing to the dragonflies. "They can turn into women."

"Women?" I asked you, fascinated.

"Yes, women. They come and get you at night in the form of insects and destroy your dreams, they put terrible spells on you, and they can even kill you . . . ," you said, opening your eyes wide.

"Why?" I cried excitedly.

"They're women who pray against you. They kneel before a cross and loosen their hair and repeat magic phrases that no one knows."

"Women on their knees . . . do you know these magic phrases?" I asked. I wanted to know them, too.

You shook your head and continued: "But I know magic phrases to chase away the *ronni ri notti*—the night women. They're the women who turn themselves into dragonflies and fly at night . . ."

"Oh, yes."

"The next morning, you know they've come because your hair is woven into tiny, almost invisible plaits that are impossible to undo."

"Impossible?" Now I could only muster single words.

"Not impossible exactly . . . you have to spray your hair with oil and recite these phrases." You took a deep breath and your huge belly swelled until it seemed about to burst. "Holy Monday, Holy Tuesday, Holy Wednesday, Holy Thursday, Holy Friday, Holy Saturday, Sunday the night women will lose their wings."

I sat there with my mouth open and whispered. "Beautiful . . ."

"And remember: every time you see a dragonfly, kill it. If you let it live, it's more likely that you will die."

We went on splashing our feet in the water while I allowed myself to fill up with the fascination of your stories.

"I hoped you would come back soon," I say to Thomas as I finish the last of the food from my empty, dirty plate.

"Sorry, I had problems at work," he replies, embarrassed.

I'm embarrassed by lies and hypocrisy, they make me feel small and insignificant, they make me slide into the certainty that the other person thinks me stupid, inferior, untrustworthy. In this case, mad.

I summon my courage and say, "Please tell me—who's Viola?"

"Who's Viola?"

"Who's Viola?" I repeat.

"Oh yeah, she's the one who let me have the dog," he says and points to the little mongrel crouched beside us, gazing up at us with those eyes that I'm seriously starting to love.

"Oh, I get it . . . and it was so important that you had to store her number on your phone?" I ask harshly.

He shrugs and says, "What's so important about that?"

I leap to my feet and react violently. "What the hell do you mean, what does it matter? It's fucking important, that's what it is!"

He shrugs again and this time his expression has changed. "OK, we've bumped into each other in the bar a couple of times, we've had a sandwich together . . . nothing more."

"I bet! Nothing more? What else would you have wanted? A sandwich and that's that? In fact I don't really see why you'd have wanted to share it with her," I say, looking into his eyes, aware that mine are exploding from their sockets.

I stare at him and imagine him looking at her, I work my way inside him and hear his thoughts, telling him over and over to leave me. At this moment he's thinking that I'm making his life difficult, but as far as I'm concerned that's the last thing I want. Right now I just want to analyze, understand, and take possession of all the security I lack. I know, I know, at any moment he's going to slam the door and he'll never come back, he'll leave me bleeding and faded on this floor, I'll gradually disappear and stop annoying him. But right now he's got to take my hands and reassure me.

As for him, he's not the kind to withdraw from a discussion. He's the kind of person who likes to reason, to make me reason, but he can't do it. He can't say, "OK, you're being a pain in the ass, so I'm out of here"—that's not his way. He stays here with me and looks at me and sometimes smiles at me without resentment. I hate his goodness, his tolerance. He makes me feel so unworthy, so wretched and pitiful, with my tendency to hide, to seek refuge, to sink my face into the pillow, to escape my problems. I'm not capable of being so self-possessed, so empathetic.

Then he takes my hands and whispers, "I love only you."

I don't believe him. Not for a moment.

Don't ask me why, don't tell me—forget it. I just don't believe him.

* * *

Then he talks to me about freedom. He says he lacks it. He says I'm tearing off his wings. How naive of me—I thought I was his freedom, that I was his wings, and that with me he'd be able to go wherever he wanted; he would have stayed perched on my back and guided me among the clouds, among the storms; together we would have looked down on buildings from on high and laughed at the stupid, impotent men struggling on the streets, dragging themselves along like sacks of potatoes.

He tells me he has the right to meet whomever he feels like and that isn't why his love will shrink. He just says, "You've got to trust me."

As for me, I have the right to die, to destroy myself, to feel my belly crumbling, to go mad and meet my ghosts, to become their puppet.

I have the right to yield to instinct. I have the right to cry and feel good as I do so. I also have the right to think that if he feels suffocated, clearly I'm no longer the delicate, flowing wave that softened and dissolved him. It means that I'm the storm now and he's alone and he can't find shelter anywhere.

Except with Viola and her normalcy.

Thirty-one

Why do you beat your red-tipped wings like that, lovely dragonfly? Settled on that white wall with your black body you look like a word on a badly written page. Why do your wings swell each time you breathe? It's as though you were brooding hatred, rancor, rage. You've settled just a few centimeters from his photograph . . . ah no, dragonfly, we don't do that. I come over to you and take his photograph and put it to my chest and you look at me, disillusioned and in tears, as I dart glances back at you, likewise full of hatred, rancor, and rage. Are you going mad now? Your flight is uneven now and imprecise; I see you're running out of breath. If I show you his photograph from a distance, what will you do, thank me?

I won't kill you, don't worry. I'd rather see you die slowly.

I know I shouldn't have slid that horrible message under the door, dragonfly, but what do you expect me to do? It's written in my blood that I must destroy everything that wants to destroy me.

Don't say anything, because you don't know anything. You don't know what it is to be abandoned, you know nothing of the battle of love. Don't you understand that each time you immerse your big green eyes in his you're stripping me of part of my life, the air that I breathe? If you take away my breath, he won't be able to love it anymore, he won't be able to smell it.

My mother, the same mother I'm talking to now, told me that dragonflies must be killed and forgotten. But I want to see you suffer a little; I want to play with your life and keep you hanging on this thin little thread, like a sadistic Fate.

I'll tell you about that time we went to the river. It was an amazing day, the rocks were sparkling and the plants showed no sign of death or decomposition, and everything was big, wonderful, strong.

I've always been used to swimming in the sea, battling with the waves, feeling that exciting fear filling me up when the blue was so dark and so deep that I couldn't see anything. I've always confronted infinite spaces, with vague horizons. I liked it, but I didn't love it. In my heart I wanted to swim in something visible, clear, with precise contours that I could see, that I could cling to.

So when Thomas suggested going to the river, I gave a leap of joy and kissed him and whispered in his ear, "Don't chicken out—today I want to know that we'll make love in the river," and he said, "We'll see," as though it were a challenge.

Our lovemaking really was lovely and joyous and playful, with the water splashing off our warm bodies in a thousand glittering droplets. And I felt like a mermaid with her Triton; we were king and queen of the water, of that lonely place, that beauty.

Or I could tell you about that time when I was in a hotel, in some remote place in South America. I felt ill and I was shivering with cold, although my body was fine and my heartbeat was regular. Without a word he drew me to him and talked to me gently, and then my tears slowly melted on my skin and made way for my smile. And then he told me that I could, that night, forget who I was, what I was for the people out there. He whispered that I was the woman he loved and nothing more, that everything else was only a silly joke.

I could tell you that I love everything about him and I wouldn't be lying.

Can you explain to me why the hell you have two little red dots on the ends of your two wings? Did you think you would pass unnoticed, did you want to show yourself off, did you want to look seductive?

When the keys rattle behind the door she understands that the time has come to go. This, I think, is just a warning.

THIRTY-TWO

In the corridor of our house was a giant stain, right beside my room. I thought it was the profile of Alfred Hitchcock, and every time I walked past it at night I started running with my eyes shut and then slipped under your covers, still shaking with fear. Or rather, first I watched you sleeping. I stood by your side of the bed and watched you for minutes at a time, moving my head as kittens do when drunk on their own curiosity. Tears came to my eyes because you filled me with tenderness, lying there like a little girl, with your serene and heedless eyelids. Then Hitchcock came back and imposed his shadow over my eyes and I fell back into darkness and desperation, in the certainty of being alone. Then I sought your warmth.

One night, as I was running with my eyes shut, I didn't notice that the door to your bedroom was closed. I ran like an untamed horse, unaware of anything, aware only of the night and its shadows. So I crashed into the door handle and bumped my eye with greater violence than anything I had ever experienced, but I pretended everything was all right so as not to worry you. I slipped as always into your bed and went painfully to sleep. The next morning the blood was dry and dark on my cheeks. As you washed my face, concerned about what had happened to me, I looked at myself intensely in the mirror, and what I saw there was a divine, saintly figure. A bleeding child, a child that quenched itself with its own mucous membranes.

THIRTY-THREE

"Have you any idea how idiotic you've been?" he says to me, without losing his temper but with his eyes moving from one side of my face to the other.

"What was I supposed to do? She's testing us," I reply.

"But testing us with whom, with what?" he says, angry now.

"With you," I snarl candidly.

"You know you're an utter maniac?" he shrieks, his voice almost as high-pitched as a woman's.

I defend what's mine.

"That poor thing came to me in tears, saying that you left a threatening message under the door of the shop! You're completely out of your mind!" he continues.

"Aha! . . . so . . . she went to see you . . . ," I exclaim furiously. "She came to see me, too, did you know that?"

"When?" he asks, startled.

"First, you tell me if you've fucked her. Or more simply: tell me if you're in love with her or what . . . ," I say, pointing a finger at his chest.

"Fucking hell! Nothing like that, but how on earth can I get you to believe me?" He's desperate and he puts his arms around me. "Why do you go on hurting yourself? Why do you think she means anything to me?"

I pull away from him and look him straight in the eyes.

"Because I can feel it," I whisper.

After an incalculable period of time suspended between silence and complete impotence, he asks, "When did she come?"

"She left just before you got here. She flew out of the window," I say, pointing to it.

"What the f—," he exclaims.

"Dickhead. I didn't kill her. She came in a different form, and I recognized her. She wanted to pull a fast one on me, the whore, but she didn't succeed," I say proudly.

He shakes his head and goes into the other room. Without a word.

Fear holds me by the hand now and my trembling never ceases. I'm trembling now as I write, I tremble when I'm eating, I tremble as I let the water flow over my body, I tremble as I look at him, as I stare at the sky, I tremble as flocks of birds make shapes and patterns in the Roman sky. I spend hours staring at them from the window, as they perform pirouettes and veer to the right and then to the left, making circles, whirlwinds, they look like hairy moles, then they plunge down, down, to the branches of the trees.

I tremble. I tremble as everything vibrates in the world, in the air. I tremble because I know that there's still life out there and I can't live it.

I need to look at the life I have inside me, that dark life, disconnected from all the others; I need to live inside myself, because outside no one can let me live. I thought he was capable of letting me live and wouldn't let me die one day at a time. But that's what he's doing, and I'd rather he killed me all of a sudden, once and for all, with a well-aimed blow.

THIRTY-FOUR

Lying on my stomach on the bed, my face suffocating in the pillow, I put my arms behind my head and slowly start to braid my hair.

"Holy Monday, Holy Tuesday, Holy Wednesday, Holy Thursday . . . ," I murmur.

I braid it slowly and diligently, taking tiny bunches of hair between my fingers.

I think that if I do this before she does, nothing will happen to me.

My body is arched, my arms hurt because of the position I have assumed, like a spider trapped in its own web.

I tress five or six bunches of hair, run my fingertip along the plait, and feel it, smooth, hard, and very small.

I tell myself that this way she can't hurt me.

But suddenly I think of him, and I think he's exposed to danger, too.

What if the dragonfly came tonight and tressed his hair? He'd be bound to her forever and I'd never be able to have him back, not even if I cut myself into tiny, tiny little pieces and slipped under his shoes.

So, at night, I will cuddle up next to him and when he shuts his eyes I will lightly, silently, braid his hair.

And he will be safe. We will be safe.

THIRTY-FIVE

That time when I grew wings and my eyes dimmed until they were sightless, his absence became inevitable.

Now I have gulped her down in a single mouthful, because she was the only thing I could eat, because nothing now can give me as much nourishment as a human being. What I want is women's flesh, the flesh of a wicked, terrible woman, a dragonfly-woman.

I am something different and dark.

I am the impalpable fog and the terrible wind that shakes the branches, I am mean and murderous jealousy, I am the love I have lost and will never regain. I am a tangle of memories and joys that have begun to rot and decompose into humus for my obsessions to grow in.

I am a huge, stretched, white sheet on which the images of my love affair are projected, and every memory becomes a source of unease, of obsession. My desire is not to distort reality; it's an inexplicable instinct to make my life difficult and unruly. In his face I see nothing but intolerance, lies, and discomfort. I can no longer think of him, imagine him happy.

I'm a bat and I've just swallowed the dragonfly. We spent hours shut up in a bell jar, which our breath made invisible. She broke off one of my wings and I licked away the blood, my tiny, red tongue healed the wound, and then my pointed teeth tore her face and I ate it. Her body was still vibrating— you should have seen it, Mamma. A body without a head, still moving, blood still flowing through its arteries. It really was a most beautiful sight, the bell jar was splashed with loads of blood, and I licked it in a sign of victory.

I have destroyed my house and upturned my memories. My antennae are too weak; my eyes are completely blind. I swallow everything I find in my way, and I don't care if I swallow him, too.

I have no more time to remember, to reinvent myself, to let the tapeworm move its body and make me a spectator of my past.

I have no more time.

Because now, I'm sure of it, nothing is the fruit of my imagination and my fear.

Now everything's real, palpable.

If my fantasies touch me now, I'm no longer afraid, because now I know that they're here to help me. They're here to let me live unscathed or else to make me live in an abyss for the rest of my life.

For me, one life has the same value as another. If he isn't here, one fate weighs as much as another.

Thirty-six

I hear his shoes stopping outside the door, silently observing, thinking, folding in on themselves and turning around, going on their way and leaving me on my own. My bed has never been so big or so depressed; it's never been so deep and wickedly comforting. I can already feel his skin brushing mine, his tears mingling with mine, and it's only a sensation, yes, a sensation, because nothing of anything that happens, nothing, absolutely nothing is real. He's writing something, bent over the desk with his eyes drowning in his heart. I feel like a tiny ant, lying on that big, terrible bed. I wish I were even smaller and transparent. I wish he could squash me once and for all. I breathlessly seek warmth from a strip of duvet; my fingertips sense that it's crumbling away and nothing is left. My body is just a piece of bloodless flesh, thrown into a refrigerated cell, waiting for someone to buy it and cook it and eat it and do with it what he will. My body alone exists and it's a fictitious one.

The mattress yields to support a weight and I pretend I haven't felt a thing.

Two blue eyes like yours look at me and smile at me. I whisper, "Mum," but she shakes her head and smiles sweetly at me.

"You've got to go," she says. "You've got to leave and you've got to understand."

I pretend I haven't heard anything.

"Look at me," she cries, shaking me, "look into my eyes."

I look at her and there are words inside. At first they're confused scribbles dripping with ink; then gradually the letters assume a concrete form and fit together into phrases. It's a letter. It looks like a woman's handwriting, young, showy writing. There's an incredible vitality in the os and the as that inflates the letters like balloons.

The letter says:

Dear Melissa,

I'm a fan of yours. I know I'm one of many, but I hope you'll read this letter, or perhaps you'll even reply, who knows.

The story you told is not my story, it doesn't belong to me. My life is different from yours, I've had different experiences, perhaps I've made bad choices, but at least they're mine and no one else's.

And yet, dear Melissa, I feel a kind of contact with you. It's as though there were a rope pulling us tightly together. There is a connection, I've worked that out, and I hope you won't think me arrogant or anything like that. I just wanted to tell you what I think. It's something very powerful, I can't explain it.

Yours,

Penelope

PS: I'm sending you a photograph. I think it's important to give a face to someone hiding behind words.

*   *   *

"So?" I ask the woman with eyes like yours. "Another one who thinks she's me. So?"

"So, you fool, this might alleviate all your suffering. Don't you understand, don't you see that the only connection between the two of you is him? The only point in common might be the love that links you to him."

"What the hell do you mean? That it wasn't Viola but that bitch Penelope who was jeopardizing my relationship with Thomas? Are you saying I'm blind, as always?"

Her eyes are sweet again and that makes me nervous. "No," she says, "she'll come after you. She doesn't yet exist in his thoughts. She'll come if you decide, if you go downstairs, open the letter, and see the photograph she's sent you. You'll be able to decide whether to survive or to die . . . and quite honestly I don't know which is worse," and she laughs, modestly putting a hand in front of her mouth.

"Shut up! Shut up . . . stop laughing. Tell me more clearly," I beg.

She composes herself and says, "Do it like this. If you want to die outright, the best thing to do is the following: you invite her over to your place one of these days, and a few hours before she turns up, you leave. You get out of there. But you really have to go for good. In the meantime make sure that he's at home, so that when she rings the bell, he's the one who answers the door, and she'll be forced to accept his invitation to come in, because she's just had a long journey . . . and that way you'll die, but at least you'll be happy. And you'll know that everything's real and nothing is imagined anymore."

I look at her again, think for a moment, bite my lip, and then whisper, "I'll go and see her."

I open my mailbox and see that the letter's there, and I don't care, I don't give it a thought. But when I see her photograph only one thought occurs to me: She's more beautiful than I am.

And my mind's made up.

Thirty-seven

I'm on the train. The landscapes of Lazio and then of Umbria run parallel to my face, but my eyes are fixed on the seat opposite mine, and I am listening to a familiar but by now an ephemeral voice.

Thomas looks at me as he looked at me some months ago, straight into my pupils, with his eyes gleaming, his nostrils twitching, and his mouth half open. He looks at me as he looked at me when my excess of life was still so feeble.

I no longer have death in my heart, because my heart has already been stripped down to nothing. Now death is advancing like a tumor; I feel it itching as it settles among my joints and muscles.

It's slow, tender, sinuous, feline. I'm not afraid. It's playing its part well; it knows how to catch human beings in its noose.

I'm abandoning him and going back to the red house on the hill, bringing his torn-up T-shirts impregnated with his smell. I don't sleep because I sense that if I did, I would never ever wake up again. I huddle up on the sofa and think, until the light's excitement has subsided; then at night I light the fire and bring tears to my eyes by fanning the flames.

I don't know what Penelope did—I wonder if she ever came. I really hope she did, so I huddle up and think of the two of them. He says, "Come on in. Melissa should be here any minute," and she says, "Oh no, I'm sorry, I'll come back later," and then he looks at her and realizes that she has beautiful eyes and a beautiful face framed by beautiful hair. But he doesn't desire her, no, not yet. She goes downstairs to wait for me, and I will never come, so she will ring the doorbell and say to him, "Listen, she hasn't arrived yet. My train has gone . . . I can take the ten-thirty," and then inevitably he will invite her up and maybe offer her a cold beer, and then, only then, will he realize, as he watches her sipping her beer, that she has the most beautiful mouth he's ever seen. And then, only then, will he decide to kiss her.

And I go to sleep.

When I heard you crying at night, before I abandoned you, I turned to face the other way and thought, Basically it's my life. I could have made it happier in the past . . . but I couldn't do it. Should I apologize?

Should I apologize?

My new snakeskins are burning too quickly.

Thirty-eight

I follow him at night as he runs about the city on a moped with Penelope's breasts pressed up against his back. I remember when we used to enjoy ourselves counting the holes in Rome, the huge crevices that pierce the streets. From Trastevere to the Esquiline we counted thirty-eight holes; from Piazza Fiume to the Cassia there were too many to count.

I stagger among the stinking narrow streets, a poodle is shitting on the steps near our apartment, the shutters are closing, the mechanics are saying good-bye to one another, arranging to meet again tomorrow, and people are walking their dogs on leads. He comes out of the door first, followed by her, and then by the dog. I hide behind the steps and watch the girl lift up her dress and climb onto the moped—she sits like Audrey Hepburn in *Roman Holiday*. Every night for three months I've gone to spy on the door of the condominium, hoping to see them come out together. I take the six o'clock train and go, and every night I wander about Rome like a junkie, except that my drug is love. People who recognize me in the street look at me and don't talk to me, and in their eyes I see that they think I'm an addict, a star hurled too soon into the galaxy, unable to find her integrity. It's true, I haven't managed to find my integrity. I'm disturbed to the marrow.

She has a beatific smile I know very well, full cheekbones, and tousled hair. He has a kind of moribund sense about him, a dirty inheritance he must bear which also smells bitter.

I'd like him to fall hopelessly in love . . . not because his well-being makes me happy, but perhaps because I enjoy the harm I am doing myself.

Five months later, I go and stand beneath the balcony and hear her moans of pleasure, and I go home and cut my skin. I carve his name and mine with a box cutter, writing what I used to write in the toilets at school: "Melissa and Thomas forever."

He will never know of my pain, because my eyes are silent dogs that follow him, foaming at the mouth.

His happiness gives me pleasure because it's the very source of my pain, the harm I'm doing myself.

That's why I'll be eternally grateful to him. Damnation.

I curse them all.

Thirty-nine

I feel the tapeworm wriggling, nestling amid my fears and becoming their high queen.

I'm still very frightened of the dark, of monsters under the bed, and of the blood that might come out of the plug hole. I see eyes in the walls, I feel hands beating against the floor, wolves howling from somewhere over in the hills.

At night the red house assumes a dark color, it turns scarlet, and I feel as though I'm in a huge pool of blood, floating in it along with my ghosts.

The pain I feel confesses things it has never confessed before.

Pain is the source of my life, the source of my imagination. To love I must first feel pain; to feel pain I must die.

So many things have changed, Mum. It really is true that life is a concentration of many lives which, all added up together, can never give you a satisfactory result.

I'm just nineteen, and yet I've lived so many lives, too many. I've lived more lives than all the characters in my stories.

I've abandoned you, I've abandoned a love that still pulses vividly. I've abandoned myself.

Mum, everything I've lived through I want to live again. I want to make the same mistakes.

I'm locked away in my room all day and the stench of cigarettes fills the air.

My dead hair scattered on the carpet, my white, tapering fingers, my yellow irises.

I think of the dragonfly, Viola, and imagine myself reincarnated in her, if I am ever reborn. I reflect that while she may not have been part of my reality, mine and Thomas's, in reality she was there. She's always been there, and she's dug a deep, deep hole inside my soul, like a wizard with a sour apple.

I sleep, I look at myself in the mirror, and I laugh. I laugh at myself, I laugh at my ghosts, I tell them to fuck off, and they start running madly all around the house. They start chanting, they tell me I'm going to die. Today Obelinda came back to see me, and she said, "Don't imagine you're going to get away with it."

"I don't imagine anything of the sort," I told her, my eyes elsewhere.

In less than a second she slipped to the foot of my bed, widened her eyes, and asked me, "Do you know what'll happen to you afterward, do you really know?"

"Will I keep you company in the other dimension?"

"No, worse than that," she replied, her pupils now covering the whole of her face. Cheeks, mouth, nose—none of it existed anymore, just the eyes.

"Worse my dear," she went on. "Don't you know what happens to those who die of love?"

I didn't move.

She touched one of my legs and I let out a shriek of pain. She burned my skin.

"What happens?" I asked with tears in my eyes.

"You'll be forced to kill the one who brought you to your death. It will be your task, it will be your purpose."

I shook my head—I didn't want to do that.

"Yes, my darling, you will. And you'll do it because it's the only way of uniting yourself with him once more. You're his demon now, and demons can only take their own favorites with them," she said.

"You mean, you couldn't?"

"If I did, I would go on being a damned soul, while he would be a free one. If you do it, drag him with you, because he must obey only you."

"I don't want him. I'll disappear forever and watch him love: that will be the damnation I deserve," I replied.

She came over to me and breathed in my face. Her breath froze my muscles.

"You stupid, spoiled little girl. You've asked for it. The other ghosts and I will hurt you so badly you'll beg us to die a terrible death. We'll finish you off."

When I was little I drew a closed semicircle on a sheet of paper. I drew a little ball on each end of the semicircle and then wrote *love* on one side and *hate* on the other.

FORTY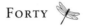

Cold floor. Doors barred and shutters lowered. Lights out. My naked body lying here. Wind on the hills. Rain. Sun. Then rain again. One week. Two weeks. Three weeks. Three days. No remorse, no kindness, no emotion. The absence of the ghosts. The sense of having attained perfection and omnipotence. Omnipotence. Omnipotence.

Then the darkness comes and grips me by the arm.

FORTY-ONE

What did you do today? When someone phoned you at six in the morning and told you they'd found your daughter lying on the floor, close to death, what did you think? Did you scream, did you curse, did you feel overwhelmed with resignation? Did you think you had a mad daughter? Or did you think you had a daughter who was passionately in love? Or perhaps both?

When you took the first flight for Rome and then traveled more than a hundred kilometers to find me, and when you reached the red house on the hill and didn't find anyone, just my hair scattered on the carpet, what did you call your pain?

What was the consistency of your love when you looked at me through the glass in the door, while my wrists, slashed and now healed, were outstretched and hanging, held up by two strips of white fabric?

What fear did you feel when you saw my eyes? When you noticed that one of them was going blind, full of clotted blood?

Would you have allowed yourself to be stroked by my hands with their shattered nails?

And that part of me I gave you, where did it end up?

If it's still inside you, free it, let it fly. Perhaps one day it will come back to me and we will have a great orgy of love.

ACKNOWLEDGMENTS

For many reasons, all different and unpronounceable, I thank the following: my dog, Burrito, who arrived late but not too late. Simone Caltabellota, who, on the other hand, arrived early. Nikki Sudden, Nic Kelman, and Rocco Fortunato. Martina Donati and Melisso, plus Nilo, the unborn child (who will have been born by now!). Julieta and Bengt, Ignacio and Mario Brega.

I'd also like to thank the coprotagonist of this story even if, in my view, I've already devoted too much time to him (both in life and in the book).

Last, I thank all the people who hate me, because it's thanks to them that I love myself all the more.